REMEMBER ROSIE

Badger Publishing Limited, Oldmedow Road, Hardwick Industrial Estate, King's Lynn PE30 4JJ
Telephone: 01438 791037

www.badgerlearning.co.uk

REMEMBER ROSIE

BEVERLY SANFORD

Remember Rosie ISBN 978-1-78464-331-7

Text © Beverly Sanford 2015
Complete work © Badger Publishing Limited 2015

Publisher: Susan Ross
Senior Editor: Danny Pearson
Editorial Coordinator: Claire Morgan
Copyeditor: Cheryl Lanyon
Designer: Bigtop Design Ltd
Printed by Bell and Bain Ltd, Glasgow

2 4 6 8 10 9 7 5 3 1

CHAPTER 1

It's definitely getting better, Lauren thought as she stacked her books in her locker. It had taken a while, but school was starting to feel easier. She even looked forward to it now, which was a far cry from her first few weeks at Brampton Academy.

"Hey – you survived double maths!" Sabrina's voice cut in over Lauren's shoulder. She turned around to see her friend opening her own locker.

"Only just!" Lauren said. She smiled shyly at Sabrina, whose sunny smile lit up her face. "I still think Mr Marks hates me, though."

"He doesn't like anyone," Sabrina laughed. "But you're getting on OK with the class, right?"

"I guess," said Lauren. "But I still feel like the new girl."

"It'll wear off," said Sabrina, slamming her locker shut. "I promise. And then you'll feel like you've been here forever."

Lauren really hoped Sabrina was right. Being the new girl was horrible. Nobody talked to you, teachers forgot your name, and you had to fend for yourself.

Her new street wasn't much different – their neighbours hadn't said more than a quick hello. Back home, everyone had known everyone else. Lauren and her friends had grown up together on the same street. They'd gone to school together, hung out in the park at weekends and grazed their knees playing football.

A pang of sadness hit Lauren and she leaned against her locker as a group of boys trampled past in their hurry to get out of school. Suddenly it all seemed a bit too much.

"Boys!" exclaimed Sabrina, noticing Lauren's glum expression. "They're always shoving about on their way to somewhere!" She tucked her arm into Lauren's. "Let's find Lexi and get out of here, yeah? I really need an ice cream. You look like you need one, too – maths is a total killer!"

Lauren was grateful. She knew Sabrina was trying to make her feel better. Sabrina and Lexi were the best things about Brampton Academy. They'd been best friends since nursery, but they still found room to let Lauren join in. She felt like a third wheel some of the time, but they always included her. Thanks to them, she'd started going out at weekends – just to the cinema or the café – and it felt great.

I just want to feel normal again, Lauren thought, letting Sabrina pull her outside.

"We NEED ice cream!" announced Sabrina at the top of her lungs to Lexi, who was waiting. "Seriously, Lex. We need to hit your mum up for a sundae before this place kills my mojo."

"Tell me about it," said Lexi. She tightened her dark ponytail and pulled a face. "I just sat through two hours of hearing about how they found King Richard's body under a supermarket car park. I'll have nightmares when I next go to ASDA!" Her eyes twinkled.

Lauren really liked Lexi. She was super smart and could cut you down with a single word. She talked really fast and sometimes Lauren couldn't understand her broad accent. "But I don't have an accent!" she'd protested when Lauren first asked her to repeat something. "You're the one with the accent, Lauren."

It stood out like a sore thumb, Lauren's northern accent. And she'd quickly learned that Londoners used different words than she did. But they'd soon started having fun with it.

Sabrina and Lexi loved saying they were 'mithered' and, in turn, they'd taught her some London words, which amused her mum and dad. Like that time she'd told Mum they should go to the shopping centre to 'have a butcher's'. Mum had been confused for hours until Lauren had explained.

Ice cream, though. There was nothing confusing about that. And a few hours hanging out with her friends at Lexi's mum's diner was perfect. "Lead the way to the mint chocolate chip!" she said, tucking her arm into Sabrina's.

*

"…I already said I was sorry," Lauren mumbled, then she winced and held the phone away from her ear. She'd taken the call outside the diner.

"For goodness sake! I was worried sick! You know the rule – let me know if you're going to be late home. I've been waiting for you to get in." Her mum was furious.

"I just forgot… I'm sorry," Lauren said. "It's not a big deal, I'm with my friends."

"Yes but I didn't know that, did I?" her mother continued. "Anything could have happened. We have to be careful, in case you've forgotten."

Lauren sighed. Of course she hadn't forgotten. And if she did forget, her mother was right there to remind her every time she left the house. She couldn't even go on the internet without being told to 'be careful'.

When they'd first moved to London, Mum freaked out if Lauren stood too near the window or if a car pulled up outside. Things were calmer now, but Lauren knew that Mum never really relaxed. She always had one eye open, keeping watch.

"I haven't forgotten. Look, I'll be home by six, OK?" Lauren said, smiling as Lexi tapped on the window of the diner. Lauren gestured to the phone and rolled her eyes. Lexi rolled her own in silent understanding.

"No, I want you to come home right now!"

"But I said I was sorry. I'm just having an ice cream with Lexi and—"

"I said NOW, Lauren."

Lauren's stomach began to knot. She hadn't heard Mum sound this angry for a long time. She felt bad then, for worrying her. She should have sent a text.

"I didn't mean to worry you, Mum. I promise I'll text you next time. But can I just stay out, please?"

Mum sighed. Then there was silence.

"Mum? Please?" Lauren was desperate not to have her afternoon ruined.

"I've told you to come home, Lauren. I'm not arguing about it."

"But Mum," Lauren wailed. "I only forgot to text you – why are you being so horrible?"

When Mum spoke, it was as though she was talking from really far away. "I'm not trying to be horrible. But I need you to come home. There's been a letter. It's about Harry."

Lauren froze.

"Did you hear what I said? There's a letter from Harry's solicitor. The appeal – it's worked. But I don't want you to worry, OK? We'll talk about it when you get home. OK?"

Lauren stood still, her fingers gripping the phone so tightly that her hand went numb. Her heart was pounding hard inside her chest, threatening to burst out. She couldn't breathe.

"Lauren? Why aren't you answering me?" Mum's voice suddenly rang out of the phone, shocking Lauren back into reality.

"I'll come home now," she said numbly.

She barely heard as Mum hung up the phone. She looked through the diner window at Lexi

and Sabrina, who were busy watching something on Lexi's phone. For a second, she thought about telling them, about confiding in her friends.

"But you'd hate me if you knew," she whispered towards the window. "I can't let you find out about Harry."

She couldn't ever let them find out that her brother was a killer.

CHAPTER 2

The past raced through Lauren's mind as she walked home. She took the long route, hoping to delay the inevitable for as long as possible.

She hoped Sabrina and Lexi believed her story. She'd gone back into the diner in a daze after hanging up on Mum, and right away they had known something was up. She'd tried to sound normal, saying Mum was just freaking out because Lauren hadn't asked permission to go out. They knew her mum was strict – she'd only recently started letting Lauren out at weekends.

But the shock was harder to hide. She was sure it had been written all over her face. The girls hadn't pushed her about it, but it must have shown in her eyes because Lexi gave her an extra-big hug when she said goodbye. She'd just

have to think of something to tell them later; a little white lie so they wouldn't dig too deep and find out the truth.

The truth. What even was that? Lauren laughed out loud, causing an elderly lady to give her a sharp look. Lauren barely felt it – she'd been through a lot worse than a disapproving look from a stranger. And it was all thanks to Harry.

Lauren kicked a tin can across the street. *Harry.* How could things have gone so wrong? They'd been really close once upon a time. She'd always relied on her older brother, known he'd look after her. But then he got in with those awful lads and everything changed. Now she hated Harry more than she'd ever thought possible.

It was little things at first. Like the time a drag queen auditioned on a TV talent show. Lauren thought she was amazing, but Harry sneered and used a word Lauren really didn't like. He did it again when they watched a famous actress thanking her girlfriend as she received an award.

"It's not right," he said each time. "We don't need that shoved in our faces, it's disgusting. It's not normal, is it?"

Lauren never knew what to say back to him.

Then there was the time he collected her from school and met her teacher, Mr Scott. Everyone in town knew Mr Scott lived with Mr Henley, who worked at the local council. Lauren never even thought about it, love was love, after all.

But Harry wouldn't shake Mr Scott's hand when they were introduced. He stood by the door, deliberately refusing to make eye contact as Mr Scott said that Lauren's guitar playing was good enough for the concert. She was really embarrassed by Harry but Mr Scott didn't seem to mind. He'd smiled and said goodbye. Harry had marched away, dusting off his jacket as if it were dirty, mumbling something under his breath.

But the first big sign came one day at breakfast when Mum was reading in the newspaper about a couple who had just got a civil partnership.

"Aww, that's lovely isn't it?" she said. "These women have been together for ten years, it's ever so nice. Shame they can't make it more official, like everyone else can."

Harry slammed the marmalade jar down on the table with such force that even Dad looked up from the sports section. "Something wrong, lad?" Dad asked.

"I don't see why that needs to be in the paper," Harry said.

"I expect they thought people would like to read some good news for a change," Mum said. "It's all hurricanes and wars and people losing their jobs all the time. It's nice to hear something positive."

"They should have their own newspaper, then," Harry snapped.

"What do you mean, 'they'?" Mum asked, looking at Dad for help.

"Them. Those sort of people. The ones who had that civil thing or whatever crap they want to call it. It's not right, you know, letting them get married." Harry's face was bright red.

"It's not a marriage, Harry," Mum said firmly. "That's the whole point. Same-sex couples can't get married yet, so they have a civil partnership instead. But they're changing the law very soon so they can marry, and—"

Harry stood up abruptly then, pushing his chair back so violently that it squealed across the floor. "It shouldn't be allowed, none of it. It's not right." He stomped out of the house, slamming the front door behind him.

Mum turned to Dad, while Lauren looked on bewildered. "Where's he getting these ideas from?" Mum said. "We didn't raise him to think like that. I bet it's those lads he's been hanging about with from the pub. I said they looked like trouble, didn't I?"

"I'm sure he's just showing off, Ellen. Trying to be the big man now he's old enough to buy a pint." Dad went back behind his paper.

Mum looked at Lauren, worry in her eyes. "I don't know what's got into him lately," she said, more to herself than anyone.

But it was only the beginning.

Harry started going out several nights a week and coming in too late for anyone to talk to him. Soon, Lauren hardly saw him any more and when she did, usually at meal times, he was distant and moody. When he was home, he stayed in his room and Lauren could hear him typing on the computer and talking to someone in a low voice.

"He's just being a lad," Dad kept saying whenever Mum said she was worried. "He's probably met a lass and doesn't want us to know." It seemed to comfort Mum, but Lauren wasn't so sure. She knew her brother better than anyone and she knew something wasn't right.

The first time Lauren heard about the EPU, she had no idea what it meant. She was unloading the washing machine and she pulled out an unfamiliar T-shirt with EPU stamped on the front in black ink, with a crudely printed image of a man with a megaphone below it. She'd never heard of EPU. She wondered if it was a rock band.

"Oi! Give me that!" Harry snatched it out of her hands; he'd come in without her hearing.

"What's EPU?" Lauren asked. "Some new band you're into? I've never heard of them."

Harry's face turned to that sneer again, the one that scared Lauren. "You will do soon," he said. "They're going to be huge."

Lauren shrugged as he disappeared back upstairs. She figured she wouldn't like the band anyway, if Harry did. But Lauren soon learned the horrible truth about EPU.

It started with the leaflets. Lauren saw them stacked on the chip shop counter one night when she and Dad were getting dinner. She recognised the image of the man with the megaphone immediately and picked it up. She gasped in shock when she saw the slogans:

SAVE YOUR CHILDREN'S FUTURE!
PRESERVE OUR ENGLISH VALUES!
JOIN THE ENGLISH PEOPLE'S UNITY!

"What's that?" asked Dad. Then he saw the leaflet. "Put that down. It's rubbish. I don't know why they've got them in here." He shoved it at the owner of the shop. "What's this nonsense, Dave?"

Dave stared at Dad. "It's a local group, Mike. You must have heard of them? It was your lad who put the leaflets in here."

"Harry did this?" Dad's face set. "Right. I'll be having a word with him. But you should think twice about having that stuff in here. It's bad for business."

"We're all entitled to our opinion…" called Dave, as Dad marched Lauren out of the shop.

That night, there was a blazing row between Harry and Dad. Mum and Lauren waited in the kitchen, wincing at the angry voices above. Then footsteps thumped downstairs and the front door slammed. Dad came into the kitchen looking weary. "There's no getting through to that lad," he said. "Says he's old enough to make up his own mind."

"Perhaps he'll get bored if we just ignore it," Mum suggested.

And so that was how it went for a few months. Nobody in Lauren's house mentioned the EPU, not even when posters turned up in town and supporters began wearing T-shirts and badges. But the day of the riot changed everything.

It started out as a happy event. Some local people were parading through town to celebrate the legalisation of same-sex marriage. It was a sunny day and the mood was fun.

But as the group neared the town hall, their way was blocked by an angry group of EPU supporters, who hurled abuse at them. The police arrived but it was too late – fights had already broken out. In the middle of the scrum a 21-year-old boy was savagely beaten to the ground. He was pronounced dead at the scene.

Mum and Lauren were at home, watching the news in disbelief, when the doorbell rang. It was Lauren who held on to Mum tightly to stop her from falling down when the police constable told her that Harry had been arrested for the murder of Mark Jones, the student who had died outside the town hall.

"Not my Harry, he wouldn't hurt anyone…" Mum wept, as she and Lauren got into the police car. But Lauren, remembering her brother's sneer, wasn't so sure.

When Harry was sentenced, Mum fainted. But the worst was still to come. The story hit the national headlines – **HARRY HARPER: TEENAGE KILLER**.

The town, in shock and mourning, turned against the family – there were bricks through the window and people threatening them in the street. Hate mail turned up in the post and Lauren was attacked on her social media accounts. Nobody cared that *they* were innocent.

Even worse, the police suspected that the EPU were behind the attacks on the house, furious that the family had given evidence against them and Harry.

Home wasn't safe any more. So, with the help of the police one rainy weekend, the family packed their things, got into an unmarked van, and moved to London. They had new names, fearful minds and troubled memories. A fresh start.

That was the day that Rosie Harper died and Lauren Cooper was born.

Rosie got left behind with the friends she'd never be able to talk to again and the house she had grown up in.

But it was Rosie Harper who put her key in the lock and stepped inside the house that suddenly didn't feel safe. It was Rosie looking through Lauren's eyes as Mum held out her arms and held her tight.

"I'm so sorry, Rosie," she whispered. "I never thought they'd let him out."

CHAPTER 3

"Earth to Lauren! Are you receiving me?" Sabrina waved her spoon back and forth in front of Lauren's face.

"Huh? Oh, sorry!" Lauren looked at her friend. "I was miles away."

"You sure were! You've been on another planet lately. I wish you'd tell me what's up."

"Nothing's up," Lauren smiled. "I'm just wondering if I should have another one of those amazing cupcakes." She pretended to concentrate on the menu, hoping Sabrina would change the subject. She hated lying to her friends but, after all, that's what her life was now – one giant lie.

"Did you ask your mum about the party? Carole really wants you to be there."

"Yeah, she says it's cool." Mum had been trying hard to make things right in the weeks following the letter. They'd not heard anything else since then, but Lauren knew that all three of them had been holding their breath, waiting to hear when Harry and his sneer would be released.

"Good, 'cos we need to pick our outfits and we need to find an amazing present. Lexi's got this idea about a collage of photos, it's so cute."

"Sounds perfect," Lauren said. Despite everything, she was really looking forward to the party at the diner. Lexi's mum Carole was celebrating her first wedding anniversary with her wife, Emma. They'd got married the day it became legal. They were going to have a DJ playing and loads of delicious food.

"I can't wait to have a dance, can you?" Sabrina beamed, glancing at her mobile phone. "Oh wow, look at this. There are some seriously horrible people in this world!" She showed Lauren some breaking news on the screen – in America a boy had been shot by another teenager simply because he was gay.

"Why did he need to shoot him?" Sabrina said, bewildered.

"Because he's different, and some people can't cope with that," Lauren said sourly, stabbing her straw into her drink. "Some people can't see beyond their own beliefs."

Sabrina raised her eyebrow. "Hmm… somebody's in a wise mood today."

"It just gets my goat, that's all. People should be free to love who they like, or believe in what they like without other people making them feel like it's wrong."

"Ah, but you're forgetting something, oh wise one!" Sabrina smiled. "Surely, even the people who believe that others shouldn't believe things have the right to believe *that* too?"

"I guess so," Lauren said. Her mind wandered to Harry – what he and his group believed in was wrong, surely? Their ideas were fuelled by hatred and disgust for anyone who was different from them. But then, they still had the right to believe those things, didn't they?

She felt more confused than ever. She wished she could talk to Sabrina about it, but that was never going to happen now, not with Harry coming out of prison.

At least I won't have to see him, she thought. That was the only silver lining. Harry had made it perfectly clear what he thought of his family when Mum had last visited him. "Don't bother coming again," he'd said, ignoring her tears. "You could have given me an alibi, you could have stood up for me, but you didn't. It's your fault I'm in here."

The visiting requests had been turned down after that, and there'd been no letters. He'd deliberately cut himself off. The letter from the solicitor had come completely out of the blue. He was representing Harry, he'd said. There was a chance that Harry might walk free because the evidence had been called into question.

None of them ever thought Harry would actually get out. It just didn't seem possible that he could get away with what he'd done. And no matter what he said, Lauren knew he'd hurt that poor boy. She just hoped that they wouldn't ever hear from him again.

*

When Lauren got home, she heard voices coming from the front room. She wondered who Mum had round – maybe a friend from work? *It'd be nice if she made some friends here too,* she thought.

She shut the door behind her and dropped her bag onto the floor.

"Is that you, Lauren?" Mum called out.

"Yeah, it's me." Lauren headed for the stairs.

"Could you come here a minute please, pet?"

Lauren sighed. She really didn't feel like being paraded in front of whoever Mum had visiting, but she opened the door to the front room anyway.

"All right, Rosie? Did you miss me, then?"

Lauren stopped dead. Harry was sitting on the sofa, legs crossed, looking perfectly at home. He had a cup of tea in one hand and a smile plastered across his face. She looked at Mum, bewildered, but Mum wouldn't meet her gaze.

"Oh, of course, it's *Lauren* now, isn't it? It suits you, sis." Harry was mocking her already, she knew it. But Mum seemed not to notice, as if she was in some sort of daze.

"What are you doing here?" Lauren finally managed to spit out.

"That's not very nice, is it? I've been locked up all this time, with murderers and wrong 'uns and all sorts, and I just wanted to see my family. I've come home, Lauren."

Lauren was appalled. She glanced at Mum, who was now looking at the floor. "How did you find us?"

Mum stood up suddenly. "I'll make some more tea," she said, slipping out of the room.

Lauren watched her go, and the truth hit her. She closed her eyes for a moment before she spoke to her brother. "That's how you knew. She told you, didn't she? She's been in touch with you all along."

And then Harry's sneer was back. "What did you expect her to do? I'm her son. She wasn't going to let me be homeless."

"Maybe you could have stayed with your *friends* back home," Lauren snapped.

Harry frowned. "Look, I just want a fresh start. I'm not here to cause trouble – I don't talk to them any more. I need to put all that behind me. Maybe we can be a family again." He stood up and walked over to her. "Can we try, at least for Mum's sake?"

It was so convincing that she almost fell for it, but then she saw the scorn dancing in his eyes.

She looked at her brother, the killer, who had just fed her a pack of lies, and then she thought about Mum and how hard it had all been for her. Without speaking, she let Harry hug her, and then she went to her room and cried silently into her pillow.

CHAPTER 4

For a few weeks, at least, Harry was a model son and brother. He helped with the housework, watched telly with Mum when Dad was working lates, and even offered to help Lauren with her homework. He rarely left the house — he said it was too soon to show his face, even though the news of his release hadn't made it as far as the national press.

"I don't want you to go through any more hell," he said to Mum when she suggested they go out for a meal. "Don't want to be recognised, do I?"

"I really think he's changed," Mum confided in Lauren the same evening while Harry was upstairs. "Maybe he'll be able to have a normal life again, get a job even." Lauren said nothing.

She knew the old Harry was in there somewhere; it was only a matter of time before he turned up.

*

"Is that you, love?" Mum called down the hall as Lauren shut the front door.

Lauren wandered into the kitchen. Mum was bustling around the cooker, looking really cheery.

"Will you want any tea?" Mum asked. "Or did you eat at the diner?"

"I'm already stuffed. We tested out loads of the food for the party – it was amazing! Miniature burgers, tiny hot dogs, cupcakes – everything. Carole and Emma are amazing cooks."

"It'll be a lovely party," Mum said. "Although I don't know how Lexi stays so slim living with two chefs!"

"What's this party then, sis?" Harry was standing in the doorway, a broad smile on his face.

"Just something at the diner, it's no big deal," Lauren said.

She bit her lip anxiously – how much had he heard? She didn't want him anywhere near that party.

"Someone's birthday?" Harry asked.

"It's Carole and Emma's wedding anniversary. Carole is Lexi's mum – you know, Lauren's friend Lexi? From the diner? Oh bother… it's boiling over…" Mum, distracted by the cooking, had spoken without thinking. Lauren saw her cringe as she realised what she'd said.

Mum didn't see the expression on Harry's face, as her back was turned. But Lauren did. That sneer was back for just a moment, then it slipped behind a cloud as Harry looked at Lauren.

"Well that sounds nice, doesn't it? When's the party?" He smiled just in time for Mum to turn around. She looked pale.

"Not for a while yet. Oh – can you set the table please, Harry? Don't forget the black pepper."

"Yeah, OK."

Lauren stared at Harry, waiting for his face to slip. But he just got on with setting the table, the smile still touching his lips. Lauren went up to do her homework, feeling confused. The old Harry would have said something nasty just then; the old Harry wouldn't have been able to keep in his disgust about Carole and Emma. Maybe Mum was right after all? Maybe Harry really had changed.

*

Things started to unravel on the day that Harry first met Lexi and Sabrina. The girls were walking out of the school gates, talking excitedly about the party. Lauren was digging in her backpack and so she didn't see the tall, blond boy leaning on the railings.

"Hello *Lauren*."

Lauren stopped so suddenly that Lexi nearly crashed into her.

"What are you doing here?" Lauren fought hard to keep her tone neutral. This was her worst nightmare – Harry meeting her friends!

"Can't I walk my sister home? Or isn't that cool down in London town?" Harry had his most charming grin on, which to Lauren's horror was already having an effect on her friends.

"OMG! You never said you had a brother," Sabrina hissed, poking Lauren with her elbow.

"I've been away," offered Harry. "Just moved down to be with the family. I'm Harry."

"I'm Sabrina," Lauren's friend beamed her biggest smile. "I can't believe Lauren didn't tell us about you!"

"Neither can I," said Lexi, from Lauren's other side. She wasn't smiling though. She was staring hard at Lauren as if to say, *what else have you been keeping from your friends?*

"So I'm guessing you must be Lexi, then?" Harry turned the charm on her like a searchlight.

"Yeah, that's right. Nice to meet you." Lexi didn't sound as if she meant it.

"I expect I'll be seeing more of you girls, then," Harry said. "I'll have to check out this amazing diner that Lauren keeps going on about."

"You should come to the party," Sabrina blurted out. "You can get to know everyone then."

Harry smiled. "I might just do that."

"We need to get moving, before the library shuts." Lexi grabbed Sabrina's arm firmly. "I'll text you later, Lauren." She gave her a meaningful look.

"Bye girls!" called Harry as they walked away. "Lovely friends you've got, Lauren."

Lauren said nothing. Her stomach was in knots, fretting about what lie she could spin to her friends to explain why she hadn't told them about Harry.

They hated secrets, Lexi especially. She'd had a rough time when her parents had split up, as Carole hadn't been able to tell Lexi about Emma. Lexi had confided the whole story to Lauren, and so Lauren felt terrible that she'd been keeping a secret from her.

The texts that she got later didn't surprise her too much.

So when were you going to mention you had a brother?

I thought we didn't keep secrets from each other.

Lauren sighed. What could she possibly say? *Hi, my brother's a horrible murderer who killed someone because he was gay. Sorry that I didn't tell you, but I didn't want to lose you.* No, she couldn't tell Lexi about Harry's past. Lexi would just think she was like Harry, like her friends back home had done. She had to lie, there was no other choice.

I'm sorry, Lex. He's been away for ages and we had a big fall out before I moved here.

I didn't really want to think about him. But it's better now.

She really hoped that would cut it. It wasn't too far from the truth, either.

OK Lauren, I understand. But no more secrets, right? You know you can tell me anything.

Just as long as I keep him away from you, Lauren thought. *If I keep you apart, then everything will be fine.*

But keeping Harry away from her friends was tricky. Sabrina kept finding excuses to pop round – she'd forgotten today's homework, or she needed to borrow a book. Lauren had hardly ever had anyone round – she'd been too worried about the truth sneaking out – but suddenly Sabrina seemed to be there all the time. She clearly fancied Harry.

Thankfully, Harry had started going out again. "To see his case worker," Mum told Lauren. "He's trying to help Harry get some voluntary work."

*

The day he turned up at the diner was the first real warning. Sabrina and Lauren were stuffing their faces with cake and giggling over a YouTube video when a shadow fell across the table.

"All right girls? Mind if I join you?"

Lauren did mind, actually, but Sabrina got in before she could speak. "Harry! Sure, you can join us, sit down." She smiled at him. Lauren cringed inwardly.

"So this is the famous diner, then." Harry looked around the place. "Very fancy, isn't it?"

He sat down and pulled the menu across, glancing at the contents.

"We like it," said Lauren.

"Where's your other friend, Lexi isn't it?" asked Harry.

Sabrina's face fell. "She's working. She waitresses here for her mum after school."

"How nice," said Harry, the sneer flickering across his face. "Keeping it all in the family."

Lauren pushed her cake away; she'd just lost her appetite.

"Aww Lauren, I thought you loved my Red Velvet cake." Carole bustled over with a mock frown, her curls dancing about behind her. "It's your favourite!"

"I'm just not very hungry," Lauren said. "Sorry."

"I hope you're not getting ill before our party," said Carole. She put an arm across Lauren's shoulders.

Harry stabbed the menu back down on the table. "My sister's fine," he said, an air of chilling calm about him.

"Ah! You must be Harry!" said Carole. "Lexi told me about you. Lovely to meet you at last."

Harry smiled politely but it didn't reach his eyes.

"Look, here's Emma, she's been dying to meet you too." Carole waved her hand at a pretty blonde woman who had just walked in. "Sweetie, come over here and meet Lauren's big brother, Harry."

"Hi Harry!" Emma smiled. "Good to meet the mysterious brother at last. Are you coming to our party? It's going to be great. We're even re-painting this place next week especially for it." She slipped her arm around Carole's waist and kissed her on the lips.

Lauren winced as Harry recoiled as though a poisonous snake was in front of him. He stood up suddenly. "Come on Lauren, time to go."

"Didn't you want anything to eat?" asked Carole. She looked from Harry to Lauren, confused.

"From here?" Harry spat the words out. "You must be joking. I wouldn't eat here if I was starving and it was the last restaurant on Earth. It's revolting!"

"Oh!" Carole exclaimed, taken aback.

"Hey, there's no need to be rude," Emma said. "If you don't want to eat here, that's fine. We understand."

Harry leaned into her face and sneered, "Do you? No, I don't think you do."

"Come on Harry, let's go." Lauren pulled on his arm. Sabrina sat still in her seat, staring at Harry in horror.

Emma stood her ground. "If you've got a problem with something mate, I'd like to hear it."

Harry laughed out loud. He looked her up and down, then jabbed the air in front of her. "*You're* my problem. You and her."

Sabrina gasped. Lauren pulled on Harry's arm again. "Please! Let's just go home."

Emma stepped forwards. "Your sister's right. It's time you left. I don't want to have to call the police."

The mention of the police seemed to calm Harry's fury. He stepped backwards, pulling Lauren with him.

"You'll keep!" he said, and then he spat on the floor in front of the couple.

As Lauren was pulled through the door, all she saw was Lexi, standing with a plate in one hand and the other over her mouth in shock.

CHAPTER 5

"I really think you should see the doctor," Mum said, feeling Lauren's head. "You don't want to miss too much school."

Lauren pulled the duvet over her head. "I just need to sleep," she lied. "It's probably a virus. Loads of people at school have had it."

"Hmm," said Mum. "Well if you need anything, Harry will be back from his appointment by eleven. I've got to get to work."

I'd rather be dead than speak to him, Lauren thought as Mum left the room. It'd been four days since the incident in the diner. Four days since she'd last spoken to him, four days since she'd talked to her friends.

She'd thought about sending Lexi a text but she was too ashamed to do it. She should have stopped him, should have stood up for Carole and Emma. *But I'm too scared,* she thought.

Instead, she'd hidden in her room all weekend, pretending she had homework. Then when Monday swung around, she'd stayed in bed and told Mum she was ill. She couldn't face seeing the girls at school.

She dozed back off to sleep, wishing she would wake up and find out it had all just been a nightmare.

*

Something woke Lauren up an hour later. It sounded like Harry. He must be back from seeing his case worker.

She didn't want to see him but she needed the bathroom, so she padded across the carpet and quietly opened her door. She was about to tiptoe past his room when she heard him talking urgently.

"Yeah… today. I've just had another look. The place is definitely closed today. There's a sign in the window about re-decorating, like they said."

Lauren paused on the landing, listening intently.

"Yeah, I know – and if we're lucky they'll both be there. Two little birds with one stone, eh?" He laughed. "A nice flaming cocktail to celebrate that anniversary?" He laughed even harder then, it was icy, harsh.

Horror crept into Lauren's heart. She knew that tone, knew that version of Harry. Cruel and cold. He'd been there all along, hiding under a mask. She had to find out what he was planning.

The floorboard squeaked and she quickly padded into her room and got right under the duvet, hearing Harry's door open. She held her breath as he came into her room and walked over. She could hear him breathing as he stood next to the bed.

"Lauren? You awake? … Lauren?"

Lauren let out what she hoped was a convincing snore. If he pulled the cover away, he'd see she was awake. She prayed that he wouldn't. Thankfully, he walked away.

Lauren breathed out as he went back to his room. Now all she could do was wait.

*

Lauren pulled on her trainers and a hoodie, grabbed her phone, and waited behind her door. Hearing him close the front door, she crept downstairs and waited before sneaking out.

The streets were quiet and she only had cars to hide behind as she followed him. He was heading for town, carrying a big, black gym bag.

A few times she thought he'd seen her, but he carried on sauntering along. As they got closer to town, she found it harder to keep track of him in the crowds. His blue hoodie kept disappearing in a sea of others.

Frustrated, she sped up as he crossed the square, but in her haste a dog lead tripped her. The owner grumbled and the tiny dog yapped, pulling her eye from her target.

When she looked up again, Harry had gone. "Oh no!" she said, scanning the square for a familiar blond head and blue hoodie. But he was nowhere to be seen.

Wandering to the north side, she realised she was thirsty so she headed for a shop just off the square to grab a drink. She didn't want to risk being seen by Mum, who worked nearby.

As she stepped out of the shop, she saw with alarm the boy in the blue hoodie waiting for her, arms folded.

"Not very good at following someone, are you?" he sneered.

"I – I wasn't…" Lauren stammered.

"Don't lie," he said, his face hardening.

"I haven't, Harry. Look, I'm skiving off. Mum thinks I'm ill. You can't tell her."

"Oh, you've got so good at lying, haven't you, Lauren? Lying to your friends, lying about your name… and now you're lying to me. I know you heard me on the phone. But it doesn't matter. You're not getting in my way. I've got something important to do."

Lauren stared at him. He looked crazy. "What are you planning?" she asked.

Harry laughed at her. "Just a little surprise, that's all. Got to show my boys I'm back, haven't I? Don't want them thinking I've gone soft just 'cos I got off." He started walking away from her.

"No!" she called out. "Please, you don't have to do anything. Just come home. The EPU aren't your friends, what they're doing is wrong. Please, Harry. It's wrong."

Harry turned around to face her. She didn't even recognise him any more, his face was so calm yet his eyes were filled with hate. "No. It's people like your friend's mother who are wrong. And them raising children, too, it's messed up. Someone has to show them that they can't get away with it. You'll thank me in the end, trust me."

Lauren gasped as the realisation sank in. "No, no, no," she said. "Harry, you can't. They're my friends."

Harry marched up to her in fury. He practically spat the words out in her face.

"They're disgusting, Lauren. And if you're going to keep defending them then you're disgusting too. My own sister, one of them. I can't even look at you." He walked off, as Lauren's eyes filled up with tears.

"Are you OK?" A kind-faced boy had stopped in front of her.

"Umm… yeah, thanks. Brothers… you know…" Lauren stumbled over the words.

"Well, that doesn't make it OK to be so horrid, does it?" The boy smiled. "Take care of yourself."

He walked away. He was young, not more than 21 or so. The same age as Mark Jones.

Mark Jones's face flashed in front of Lauren's eyes. Mark, the peaceful student, who would have been enjoying life today, like this lad, if Harry hadn't killed him. And suddenly she knew what she had to do.

The phone rang out to voicemail every time Lauren tried to call Lexi. It was lunchtime; she knew Lexi would have her phone with her. Desperately, she tried again but the phone cut off mid-ring. And then she knew that Lexi didn't want to talk to her.

Scrolling through her contacts, she called Sabrina instead but it went straight to voicemail. She swore, and waited what felt like hours for the voicemail message to end before leaving her own:

"Sabrina – listen to me – you need to warn Lexi. Tell her Carole and Emma mustn't go to the diner today. You've got to tell her NOW. It's Harry. He's a killer, he's with the EPU. I'm calling the police. There's no time to explain – just please stop them from going to the diner!

"And it's me, Lauren, by the way – no, that's a lie. My real name is Rosie, Rosie Harper."

CHAPTER 6

When the petrol bomb hit the diner, the glass flew everywhere. The street outside looked like it was covered in glittering ice.

The police arrived soon after, then the fire engines and ambulances. Lauren stood numbly to one side, as an innocent passer-by, caught up in the blast, was stretchered away, blood on their face.

She'd been too late. She hadn't stopped him. She stared at the diner, praying desperately that Carole and Emma weren't somewhere in the burning wreckage.

Harry was alive. He'd been pulled away from the diner by the police, grinning insanely as blood streamed down his face. He looked like he was crying blood. He sneered at Lauren as he got into the ambulance, cuffed tightly.

"He didn't even deny it," Lauren heard one woman say. "He just let the police take him."

"That's how it is with those kind of people," a man said. "They don't think what they're doing is wrong."

"Well, it's not right!" the woman said.

Lauren shook her head at the familiar words. She wished Mum would hurry up and get here.

"Lauren?" a familiar voice spoke from behind her. She turned to see Lexi standing there, her eyes filled with tears.

"Oh my God – Lexi…!" Lauren burst into tears. "I'm so sorry, I tried to stop him. I really tried."

"No, it's OK, shhhh, listen," Lexi's smile was kind. "Mum and Emma were on the way here when Sabrina got your message. Because of you, they didn't come. You saved their lives. You saved my mum's life, Lauren."

"They're OK? Really?" Lauren cried even harder with relief. "Lexi… I'm so sorry about everything. I never wanted to lie to you. It was Harry – what he did when he killed that boy. We had no choice, we had to start again. Everyone blamed us... they thought we were like him."

"I would have understood," Lexi said. "You should have trusted me."

Lauren was suddenly exhausted. The pain of her secret was falling away, but the uncertainty of her future weighed down on her. "I didn't think you'd want to be my friend any more," she whispered. "If you knew."

"Oh Lauren," Lexi pulled her into a hug. "I know better than anyone what it feels like to be judged – look at my family." She smiled. "Of course I want to be your friend, silly."

"Really? You mean that?" Lauren smiled through her tears.

"But there's just one thing – what do we call you now? If you're not Lauren?"

"Rosie," Lauren said. "My name is Rosie."

THE END